Magic Carpet

Stories from around the World

Magic Carpet
Stories from around the World

The Boy who Served his Tribe

a myth of the Chippewa people of
North America

Retold by
Frances Usher

The Palm Tree and the Banyan Tree

a tale from
Vanuatu in the South Pacific

Retold by
Janie Hampton

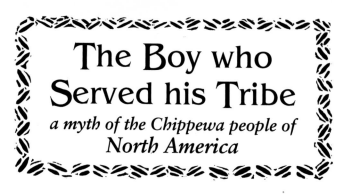

The Boy who Served his Tribe

a myth of the Chippewa people of North America

Retold by
Frances Usher

L ong, long ago, there was a family of the Chippewa tribe, who lived in a wigwam in the woods of North America.

Mother and father, brothers and sisters were all very happy and contented, for they loved the good things of the Earth. They loved the sunshine, the forests and the cool springs of water. But they were often cold and hungry, for at this time the Chippewa people did not know about growing corn. Instead, they lived only by hunting.

Now, when boys of this tribe reached the age of fourteen, it was the custom for them to go into some lonely place, without food, so that they could be alone for several days and think about the life which lay ahead of them.

The time came for the eldest son of the family to carry out this custom.

"Come with me, my son," said his father.

The two of them walked far into the woods together. There, the father built a little wigwam for his son.

"You will be here for seven days without food," he told the boy. "At the end of that time, I will return for you and bring you food. While you are here, you should pray to the Great Spirit that he will send you a gift. A gift for the whole tribe."

Left alone, the boy sat for a time and thought. What should he pray for during this week's fast?

Perhaps he should pray that his tribe would win glory in battle. Or should he pray that they would enjoy good hunting, or be sent great wealth?

No, he thought. He would ask only that life for his tribe might be made in some way a little less hard.

And so he began to pray to the Great Spirit.

A day passed, and another. The boy continued to pray, and he ate nothing.

By the time the third day came, he was weak from lack of food. All he could do now was to lie inside his wigwam in a kind of dream.

All at once, the curtains of the wigwam parted, and a young warrior entered. The plumes of his head-dress were green, and so were his moccasins and his cloak. When he spoke, his voice was like the rush of the wind through the trees.

"The Great Spirit has heard your prayers," the warrior said to the boy. "I have come to test your courage. Stand up."

Trembling a little, the boy stood up.

"Now wrestle with me," said the stranger.

And so the two of them began to wrestle, and they struggled together for a long time in silence.

At last the warrior said, "That is enough for today. I will come back tomorrow."

The next evening, the curtains of the wigwam parted again, and the warrior was back. Again, the boy wrestled with him. And although he had felt so weak before the stranger came that he could scarcely stand, as soon as he touched the green-plumed warrior he became strong.

"Good," said the warrior at the end. "You have done well. I will come back tomorrow."

And so, each evening, it was the same. The stranger in the green head-dress and moccasins and cloak came, and the boy's strength returned as soon as he touched him. Each evening, they wrestled.

By the seventh evening, the boy was utterly exhausted from lack of food. When the stranger came in, he managed to pull himself to his feet. As usual, the two of them began to wrestle.

Once again, as soon as they came to grips, the boy felt his strength come back.

"It's strange," he thought, "but tonight I think I could even throw this stranger to the ground."

So well did the boy wrestle, that indeed he threw the man to the ground.

The boy knelt down by his side. To his utter horror, he saw that the warrior was about to die.

The man smiled at him.

"You must not be sad," he said, "and you must not grieve for me. You shall see my green plumes again. But if you wish to see them, this is what you must do.

"Bury me, and keep my grave covered with fresh, damp earth. When I have slept a good sleep, I will break through the earth and return to the sunshine."

So the warrior breathed his last.

With a heavy heart, the boy carried out all his instructions.

No sooner had the boy finished burying the stranger, than he looked up and saw his father coming towards him through the woods.

"See, my son, I have come to fetch you," said his father, "and I have brought you food. Eat and your strength will soon return."

And when the boy had eaten and regained his strength, they went home together to the family, and to everyday life.

But the boy did not forget his friend with the green plumes, and he never forgot to visit the grave and to weed it and water it.

The boy told nobody about what he was doing, not even the members of his own family. He was afraid that, if he told people about the warrior and his visits, they would say that he had dreamed it all because he'd been so weak from lack of food.

Then, one day, the boy was coming home from a week's hunting trip, and he decided to visit the warrior's grave.

As he came near it, he saw that something was different. The fresh clean earth of the grave was covered in green plumes! He went nearer.

"Not plumes," he said to himself softly. "Leaves. Wide, pale, green leaves."

He stood there, staring at them. He had never in his life seen leaves like them, and he did not know what to do.

Should he tear them out?

"No." He shook his head, remembering how the young warrior had died, his eyes fixed on the boy's own. "He told me to trust him, and I will."

Weeks passed, and the boy went on watering and weeding the warrior's grave. The green shoots pushed up through the earth and became tall, strong plants. At last the day came when golden tassels swung from them, thick golden tassels. Then the boy knew that it was time to fetch his father to see them.

The older man stood silently at the side of the grave, while the boy explained the whole story. At last the father spoke.

"My son," he said, "this is a gift from the Great Spirit. A gift to all the Chippewa people."

The boy looked puzzled.

"A gift?" he asked. "What is it, father?"

The man reached out and touched the golden tassels gently. He took a few grains from them and tasted them. Then he turned and looked at the boy, and his face was as glad as the morning sun in the sky.

"It is a new kind of food, my boy," he answered. "The Great Spirit has sent us food that will grow where we plant it in the earth. From now on, we Chippewas will not need

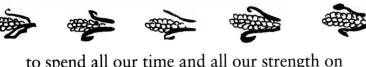

to spend all our time and all our strength on hunting animals in the forests."

The boy's father was right. By his death, the warrior had taught the Chippewas how to grow corn. In time, they harvested it and made bread for themselves. And so their lives were made a little less hard, just as the boy had asked of the Great Spirit in his prayers.

The Palm Tree and the Banyan Tree

a tale from
Vanuatu in the South Pacific

Retold by
Janie Hampton

On an island in the South Pacific Ocean grew two trees. One was a coconut-palm tree, and the other was a banyan tree. When they were young they were about the same size and they were quite friendly. They talked about the tide coming in and out, and the sun rising and setting. Occasionally there was a hurricane, or even an earthquake. But the trees preferred to talk about the good things, and not the frightening and dangerous ones.

As the tides came and went, and the sun rose and set, the trees grew taller. Or at least the palm tree did.

14

When the palm tree grew its first coconut, it was very proud.

"I am a very clever palm tree," said the palm tree to the banyan tree.

"What makes you so clever?" asked the banyan tree.

"Look what I have done – I have grown a coconut. The fruit is sweet and tasty. Now everyone will want to be friends with me. You'll see."

Soon a crab came scuttling along the beach, its shell clanking against the pebbles.

"Crab," called the palm tree. "Would you like to eat my coconut? The fruit is very sweet and tasty."

"Well, that does sound fine," said the crab. "But how shall I eat it?"

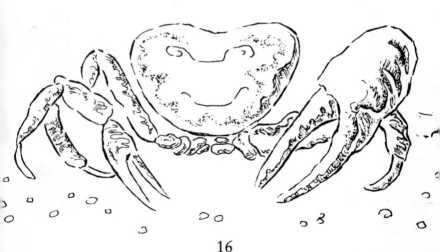

The palm tree shook itself, but nothing happened; the coconut just stayed put at the top.

"Might I make a suggestion?" asked the banyan tree. "Crab, you climb up the trunk and break off the coconut stem with your claws. Then the coconut will fall down and split open."

So the crab climbed up the trunk of the palm tree, and with its sharp claws it sawed through the stem of the coconut.

The coconut fell down with a crash. It split open. The crab climbed carefully down again and bit into the soft, sweet flesh of the coconut.

"Yes, I have to agree that you have grown a very tasty coconut," said the crab, smacking his lips.

"I told you I was clever," said the palm tree to the banyan tree. "Even the crabs think so. My coconuts will be famous the world over."

The banyan tree did not answer. There didn't seem any point in mentioning the small berries it was growing on its short stubby branches.

One day a small boy with a large knife came along.

"Did you know that I grow the best coconuts on the island? They are very sweet and tasty," said the coconut palm. "Would you like one?"

"Yes please," said the boy.

"Well, climb up and choose the biggest."

The boy put his knife between his teeth and hitched up his shorts. He grabbed the trunk with his hands and gripped the bark with his bare feet as he climbed up the tree. At the top he chopped away at the branches and a shower of coconuts fell down.

"I didn't mean you to cut them all down!" said the palm tree, as the coconuts bounced to the ground.

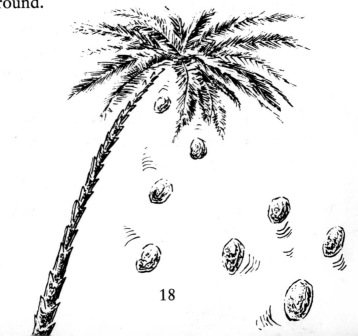

"Watch out!" shouted the banyan tree. "You'll squash me."

"You're just too small," laughed the palm tree.

The boy scrambled back down the tree and ran off with as many coconuts as he could carry.

The tides came and went, the sun rose and set, and the palm tree grew taller and taller.

The banyan tree grew too. It didn't grow up, but it grew out, and new roots grew down from the branches. When they touched the ground they became more trunks. All the branches held hands with each other, until it was impossible to see the middle of the tree. Leaves sprouted everywhere and berries ripened on the end of every twig.

"Every day in every way I grow more beautiful," the palm tree said.

"Oh, and why is that?" asked the banyan tree.

"Because I am tall and straight," said the proud palm tree. "I can see a very long way, and I don't take up too much room."

"Yes, I have to agree there," said the banyan tree, who didn't like to get into arguments.

"What's so special about being tall and straight?" the banyan tree wondered to itself. It was beginning to feel just a bit grumpy about the coconut tree's proud boasts.

One day the palm tree saw the crab scuttling along the beach.

"Come and eat my coconuts," the palm tree called to the crab. The palm tree was always trying to find someone to talk to.

"No thanks," said the crab. "Your coconuts are indeed delicious. But the trouble is, if I eat them it will make me taste so good that everyone will want to eat me. That's what has happened to a lot of my family, and now there are very few of us crabs left. So I'll stick to eating banyan berries, thanks all the same."

The crab wandered over to scratch among the leaves under the banyan tree for berries.

"Hello," said the crab quietly to the banyan tree. "These berries may be small, but they are much easier and safer to eat than coconuts."

"Thank you," said the banyan tree. "You are very welcome to come and eat them whenever you want. I won't disturb you. Enjoy your meal."

Another day the palm tree saw the little boy, who was playing with some friends.

"Come and climb my trunk," the palm tree called to the boys.

"No thanks," said the boys. "You are too tall to climb now. And you only have one straight trunk to climb. My friends and I prefer to play in the banyan tree – it is much more fun."

The boys climbed in and out of the intertwining trunks. They chased each other from one part to another, trying not to touch the ground. The banyan tree was happy to have so much laughter around it.

High noon came. The sun was hot, and the palm tree was beginning to wilt.

"Come and sit under me," called the palm tree to a passing dog.

"No thank you," said the dog. "Your trunk is too thin and straight – you give very little shade. I prefer to sit here."

The dog wandered over to lie under the roots of the banyan tree.

One evening, when the sun was beginning to set and the air had cooled, the palm tree saw a great turtle coming up out of the sea on to the sand.

"Come and lay your eggs under my tree," said the palm tree to the turtle.

"No thank you, your leaves are too spiky," said the turtle.

The turtle found a sheltered spot among the soft leaves under the banyan tree. She dug a hole with her back legs and laid her eggs. Then she covered them up so that no one could see them.

"Would you mind keeping an eye on my eggs until they hatch?" said the turtle to the banyan tree.

"Of course I will," agreed the banyan tree. "And when your little turtles hatch, I'll point them towards the sea."

It was a clear crisp morning when the blue pigeon landed on the palm tree.

"Come and make your nest in my branches," said the palm tree to the blue pigeon.

"No thank you," said the blue pigeon. "Your branches wave around in the wind too much. I'll make my nest among the sheltered branches of the banyan tree."

Later that day some women came to wash their clothes in the sea. They slapped them against a smooth rock and wrung the clothes dry between them.

"Come and hang your washing on my trunk," called the palm tree to the women.

"No thank you," they said. "Your trunk is too straight. The banyan tree has lots of horizontal branches to hang our washing on."

The banyan tree was soon covered in brightly coloured shirts, trousers and skirts.

The palm tree was getting grumpier and grumpier. It knew that it was the most beautiful, straight and tall tree on the island, but nobody wanted to listen. They all went to the short, fat banyan tree.

"Don't you just love the evenings when the boats come home and the sun sets behind them?" said the banyan tree, trying to ignore the palm tree's bad mood.

"It's not a bad sight," said the palm tree, "but of course I can see it much better than you."

"I can see it all very well, thank you," said the banyan tree.

"You have too many leaves getting in the way. You are such a mess – all leaves and branches," said the palm tree. "I am tall and straight and beautiful. I am the most beautiful tree on the island."

"Well that's as may be," said the banyan tree, who was getting cross and really did not want to continue the conversation.

That evening the sun disappeared much earlier than usual. The sky was dark and the tides did not go out. A terrible wind began to blow. The waves grew bigger and crashed higher up the beach.

"This is really scary," said the banyan tree. "The wind is blowing so hard that I'm losing half my leaves."

"You are so feeble," said the palm tree. "Can't you even stand up to a hurricane? I am tall and straight and beautiful. No hurricane can frighten me."

The wind blew and blew. Banyan leaves and twigs were ripped from the branches which bent and twisted. The blue pigeon sat tight in her nest among the small branches.

The crab and the turtle came scuttling up the beach together.

"The sea is too rough for us today," said the turtle.

"Come and shelter beside me," said the palm tree.

At that moment some coconuts came crashing down.

"Watch out!" shouted the crab. "We'll be much safer with the banyan tree." And they crouched among the soft leaves and roots.

The boy and his friends came running along the beach.

"Come and shelter under me," said the palm tree.

"No thanks, we'll be safer inside the banyan tree," they said. "You have too many coconuts which may fall on our heads."

The children climbed right inside among the branches and peeped out to watch the hurricane blowing around the island.

The coconut tree stood tall and proud as the hurricane blew harder and harder.

"I am the most beautiful tree on the island," it shouted above the wind.

Suddenly there was a terrible crack. The top of the palm tree broke right off.

The banyan tree looked up. The turtle and the crab peeked out. The children stared.

The palm tree had been too tall, too thin, too spiky and too straight. And too proud.

But everyone liked to be around the friendly banyan tree.

The Gay
Goss-hawk

from Scott's Minstrelsy of the
Scottish Border

Retold by
Theresa Breslin

This is a story from the Scottish borders. Many traditional tales of long ago involve the gallant hero rescuing the fragile maiden. In this story the heroine, Jean, decides to rescue herself.

Jean of Mortonhall was in love with William of Aikenwood, and William of Aikenwood was in love with Jean. Good and well, you might think, but you would be wrong. For Aikenwood lay just north of the Border in the wild beautiful countryside of bonny Scotland, while Mortonhall was a few miles south of the river Tweed in the fair sweet land of England. And at the time of this story the English and the Scots did not get along together at all.

Now this was due to all sorts of reasons. They ran off with each other's livestock and set fire to each other's castles and keeps. The Border reivers rode up and down the Border plundering and fighting and stealing sheep, and generally behaving badly and causing trouble. Who was the most to blame was anyone's opinion, so I'll leave it up to yourself to be the judge of that.

reivers: people who raided farms and villages, stealing from the people who lived there.

Jean's father, the Earl of Mortonhall, had eight pretty daughters. He had strictly warned them that UNDER NO CIRCUMSTANCES were any of them even to smile at a Scotsman, far less talk to one. Never in their lifetime would he allow them to visit Scotland, and he said he would kill any Scotsman who entered through his gate.

This caused Jean, who was the youngest and
prettiest, much distress and unhappiness. Many
months previously, when riding out with her
sisters, she had lost her way and wandered over
the Border into the Aiken Wood. She had
stopped to allow her horse to drink at a little
burn and there she had met William. The two of
them had at once fallen deeply in love.

William of Aikenwood was a fine hunter. He rode out each day with his hounds and his horses, his goss-hawk sitting proudly on the leather gauntlet on his left arm. Now this hawk had very special powers. As well as being a swift and deadly prince of the skies, it could think and talk almost as well as some humans. Indeed, in some cases, better. And it wasn't long before the bonny bird noticed that its master was pining away.

"What ails thee, sire?" asked the clever goss-hawk. "I see that thy mind is not on the hunt today."

"That is true, my bonny bird," said William sadly. "Neither my mind nor my heart is with thee this morn. They are far, far away across the Border with my own dear Jean." He sighed heavily as he thought of how they could never be together. "I cannot even speak to her," he went on. "I am not allowed within sight of her, yet I want to tell her how much I dearly love her and wish to marry her."

The bird turned its bright black eyes on William. "Give me thy message," it said. "Tuck it under my wing and I will fly straight and sure with the wind to thine own true love."

35

The Lady Jean was sitting in her flower garden with her seven sisters when a strange bird came and settled in a birch tree close by. Jean watched this bird as it began to sing. First, it sang sweet and low, then loud and clear, and as it sang she thought she heard it say her name over and over.

"*Jeanie,*" trilled the bird,

"*Jeanie, Jeanie,*
Fairest flower o' England, Jeanie
Bend thy head and list to me.
Jeanie, Jeanie, bonny Jeanie."

She stood up, left her sisters and came towards the branch.

"Why do you speak my name so?" she asked, and she stretched out her hand.

The goss-hawk fluttered its feathers and William's message fell to the ground. Jean read his letter telling her that he would wait for her at St Mary's Kirk, where they would be wed. He wrote that he hoped she would come to him and that he would wait for her until the end of time.

Jean thought for a moment and then smiled a merry smile.

"Tell your master I will be there," she said.

Straightway she went to see her father.

"Father," she spoke up bravely, "you would never allow me to spend my life in Scotland, but would you let me spend my death there?"

"Daughter," he replied, "I do not understand your question."

"It is not a question that I ask of you," Jean replied, "but a boon that I beg. Grant me this wish. When I die I should like to be carried forth from here and laid to rest in St Mary's Kirk."

Her father laughed loud and long. "I fear it is you who will first see me at rest," he said, "but if it pleases you, then I will grant your wish."

Jean then spoke to her sisters. "If I should die," she said, "will you make me a shroud of the finest cloth? Also, to mark my passing I would like each of you to fasten a little silver bell upon it."

Her sisters tried to laugh away her gloomy thoughts but finally promised to do as Jean had asked them.

Then Jean hurried through the castle halls to her chamber. There she prepared a sleeping potion and drank it down. Her eyes closed, her cheeks turned pale and everyone thought she was dead.

Her sisters came and stood over her. They could not rouse her. Then they lamented sorely at the loss of their youngest sister, but in keeping with her last wishes they sewed her a white linen shroud and each of them stitched a silver bell to the side.

The next morning they laid her on an oaken bier and carried her over the Border into Scotland. As the sad procession wound its way slowly to the Kirk of St Mary, all the little silver bells tinkled one by one, just as Jean had planned.

Deep in the surrounding forest, William of Aikenwood heard the bells ringing. He stretched out his arm and his faithful goss-hawk flew down to rest upon his wrist. Together they rode on to St Mary's Kirk.

When the funeral party left, William slipped
quietly into the tiny chapel. He strode down the
aisle and gazed at his beloved Jean. Her face was
as white as the lily flower and her cheek as cold as
the snow on the Border hills. He knelt beside her
and took her hand gently in his own. Then the
rosy colour came back to her face and lips. She
opened her eyes and smiled at her gallant.

"I have waited long for you, my love," said the Lady Jean.

"And I for thee," said William of Aikenwood.

Anansi's Rocking Horse

a traditional story from
the Caribbean

Retold by
Andrew Matthews

A long time ago, people and animals were the same.

In those days, Tiger was a handsome fellow with a fine, striped coat. Tiger was very proud of himself and spoke in a loud voice, as though everything he said was worth listening to. Everyone was a little bit afraid of Tiger because he was so strong; everyone except Anansi, the spider.

Anansi was small and thin. He limped when he walked and he had a whispery voice. He had a way of slipping himself into shadowy corners where no one would notice him. Anansi wasn't strong, but he was cunning, and he liked nothing better than playing tricks on proud Tiger.

In the same village as Tiger and Anansi lived a beautiful young woman named Selina. Her smile shone like the moon and her laugh was brighter than butterflies' wings. Tiger fell in love with Selina and wanted to marry her. When he found out that Anansi also loved Selina, Tiger laughed his growling laugh.

"Anansi stands no chance with Selina!" he said scornfully. "What young woman would even look at a wretch like him while I'm around?"

Now Anansi was building a web in a quiet corner nearby, and he heard what Tiger said. His little eyes flashed with anger. "No chance, hey?" he said. "I'll soon see about that!"

Anansi went straight round to Miss Selina's house and they sat talking on the porch, sipping cool mango juice.

"People have been saying that Tiger wants to marry you, Miss Selina." Anansi said slyly.

"I never listen to gossip, Mr Anansi," replied Selina, turning up her nose.

"Well if he asks you, you must be sure to say no," said Anansi. "A respectable young lady like you can't possibly marry an old rocking horse."

"What do you mean?" gasped Selina.

"When I was little, my father paid Tiger to let me ride him like a rocking horse," said Anansi.

"I don't believe it!" Selina said.

"Then I'll prove it to you," said Anansi, and off he went to his house.

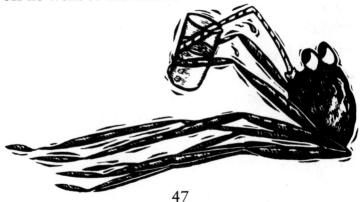

All day, Selina thought about what Anansi had said. She was a vain young woman, and the idea of marrying someone's old rocking horse made her shiver.

That evening, Tiger came to see Selina. As soon as they were alone, he asked her to be his wife. To his surprise, instead of looking pleased, Selina frowned.

"I'm sorry, Mr Tiger, but I can't marry you because you used to be Mr Anansi's rocking horse," she replied. "If I married a rocking horse, people would laugh at me."

Tiger's eyes glowed like green fire. "Who told you these lies?" he demanded.

"Anansi himself," said Selina. "He told me he could prove it."

"He'll sing a different song when I get hold of him!" snarled Tiger.

Tiger hurried round to Anansi's house and banged on the door. "Come out, Anansi!" he roared. "I'm going to make you tell Selina the truth. Rocking horse, indeed!"

The door opened slowly, and there stood Anansi. He looked pale and his legs trembled.

"Oh, I'm ill! I feel so sick!" he groaned. "I'll do anything you ask, Tiger, but please don't roar again. It makes my head ache!"

Anansi looked really ill and Tiger lowered his voice.

"Come with me to see Selina this minute, you lying rascal!" he said.

"Ooh, I couldn't possibly walk all that way!" moaned Anansi. "If you want me to go with you, you'll have to carry me on your back."

"Oh, very well!" sighed Tiger.

Anansi climbed up on to Tiger... and fell straight back on to the ground. "I can't stay on!" he whimpered. "Find a bit of string and tie it round your neck so I can hold on to it."

"Oh, very well!" grumbled Tiger.

"And fetch me that stick over there. I must have something to brush the flies away from my face!" whined Anansi.

Tiger got the string and stick, and soon they were trotting along the main street. It was a fine evening and the villagers were out on their porches. They all saw Tiger with Anansi on his back.

When they came close to Selina's house, Anansi suddenly sat up straight. He pulled on the string, kicked his heels into Tiger's sides and whacked Tiger's behind with the stick. "Gee up, Tiger!" Anansi cried. "Look, Miss Selina, I told you Tiger used to be my rocking horse – now he's my rocking horse again!"

Selina and the other villagers burst out
laughing. Tiger was so ashamed that he ran right
past Selina's house and hid in the forest. Anansi
hopped off Tiger's back and climbed to the top of
a palm tree where Tiger wouldn't find him. He
stayed in the tree for a week, chuckling about how
he got his own back on Tiger.

So Selina didn't marry Tiger – but nor did she marry Anansi. While he and Tiger were hiding, Peacock asked Selina to marry him and she said yes.

Tiger was far too proud to go to the wedding, but Anansi did. In fact, he persuaded Selina and Peacock to make him Guest of Honour.

"After all," he told them, "if it hadn't been for me, Miss Selina might have married Tiger!"

The Sweetness of Salt

a traditional story from
Pakistan

Retold by
Susan Lacy and Zahida Shah

Once there was a king who thought he was the most important person in the whole world. He never tired of telling everyone how handsome he was, how generous, how intelligent. He boasted of his greatness as a ruler and would only have people around him who agreed with him and flattered him.

Now the King had three beautiful daughters. One day he decided to test how much they loved him. He put on his golden suit, placed his crown upon his head, sat on his jewelled throne and called them to him.

"My dear daughters," he said, "everyone knows that I am the greatest king that ever lived. All my people love me and would die for me if I asked them. Everywhere I go they sing my praises and bow down before me." He crossed his arms over the rubies that sparkled on his chest.

"Now," he went on proudly, "I want to know what my daughters think of me. Tell me, each one of you in turn, how much do you love me? What is your love like?"

His eldest daughter bowed before him. "Father," she said. "I love you very much. My love for you is like honey, rich and golden."

The King smiled and nodded, greatly pleased. Then his second daughter bowed before him.

"Father," she said, "I love you very much. My love for you is like sugar, sweet and sparkling."

The King was overjoyed. Then he looked at his youngest daughter. She bowed silently before him and not a word passed her lips. "Well, come on, speak up," said the King. "How much do you love me?"

His daughter looked up. "Father," she said. "I love you just like a daughter should love her father."

"But how much do you love me?" demanded the King. "What is your love like?"

The third princess thought for a while and at last she said, "Father, my love for you is like salt."

"Salt?" thundered the King. "Your love for me is only like salt?"

"Yes, Father," she said.

"How dare you," roared the King. "How dare you? Salt. Is that all your love is worth, salt? You'd better change your mind or it will be the worse for you!"

"But Father," said the princess sadly, "what I have said is the best way to show my love for you."

The King stood up. He was in such a fury that his moustache quivered and his face grew purple with rage. "You will pay for this," he said, and with that he turned and marched angrily out of the room.

From that day on, the King acted as if his youngest daughter did not exist. He married his two elder daughters to princes and gave them each a handsome dowry. One day the queen came to him and asked him to find a husband for his youngest daughter as well.

"Who would want to marry a stupid girl
like that?" said the King. He thought for a while
and then he smiled. "Very well, I will find her
a husband."

The King went out into the street. The first
person he saw was a young man dressed in rags.
The King beckoned to him. "What are you doing?"

"I am begging for food," said the young man.
"I have had no work for many days now and I
have no money."

"Ha ha," said the King. "So you are a beggar.
You will do nicely. How would you like to marry a
princess? Then you can both beg together."

57

So the King married his daughter to the beggar
and sent them on their way without a penny. The
King's daughter was a brave girl and accepted her
fate silently. She was not sorry to go for she knew
that she was no longer a princess. The two young
people walked down the road together and as
soon as the palace was out of sight the girl asked
her husband who he was.

"I'm not really a beggar," the young man said.
"I came to this city looking for work. I only
begged for food because I had no money."

The two wandered far away from the city and
found a small hut in which to live. The young man
was hard working and, with such a brave girl as
his wife, he was ready to do anything to make his
fortune. Now the girl was still wearing some of the
jewellery that she had worn when she was a
princess so, with her permission, the young man
sold it and bought a small plot of land.

Every day, from morning till night, the young couple worked on their land. When harvest time came around, they made so much money from selling their crops that they were able to buy another plot of land. Every year they worked harder and harder, until soon they became the owners of a fine house. Not satisfied with this, they worked harder still, until after a few more years, they owned a wealthy estate. Then the young man and his wife had a sumptuous palace built with beautiful gardens all around.

By this time they had become well known in the city. All the wealthy lords and ladies invited them to their homes.

One day the couple decided to invite all the most important people to a party. They invited the girl's father, the King, as well. The King accepted the invitation, not knowing that he was going to the palace of his own daughter.

On the day of the party, servants ushered the king and all the other guests into a vast dining room. Music was playing softly, and the sweet scent of roses hung on the air. The young man and his wife welcomed their guests, and showed them to their seats one by one.

The girl looked beautiful. She was dressed in a bright red sari, with golden flowers around the hem. Over her face she wore a golden veil, and as she approached her father, she lowered it slightly and asked him to sit at the top of the table, ready for dinner.

The King sat down. On the table in front of him were several golden bowls, each filled with food of different kinds. There was spicy chicken and savoury lamb, rice with meat and rice with vegetables, creamy yoghurt and fruity chutney, and the King's mouth watered as he smelled each one. The King was hungry. He took a mouthful of food from one of the bowls and ate it greedily. Then he pulled a face. There was something wrong.

He tried another bowl. There was something wrong with that dish too. What was it, he wondered. He licked his lips thoughtfully and then he knew. *Honey.* The food had been cooked with honey. He tried another bowl. Then another and another. Every dish had been cooked with honey. Sweet, sickly honey. The king was angry. He looked around the room at all the other guests. Everybody else was enjoying their food.

Then his daughter approached him, her face still covered by a golden veil. "Your Majesty," she said gently, "you've hardly eaten anything. Don't you like the food?"

"*Like it?*" he roared. "Of course I don't like it. It has been cooked with honey." He stood up as if to go. "How dare you give a king such food. You have insulted me!"

"Your Majesty, please don't go. Try the dishes on this table instead." His daughter beckoned to the table next to his and the King sat down begrudgingly.

He took a mouthful of food from one of the bowls and ate it greedily. Then he pulled a face. There was something wrong.

He tried another bowl. There was something wrong with that dish too. What was it, he wondered. He licked his lips thoughtfully and then he knew. *Sugar.* The food had been cooked with sugar. He tried another bowl. Then another and another. Every dish had been cooked with sugar. Sweet, sickly sugar. The king was very angry this time.

Then his daughter approached him again, her face still covered by the golden veil. "Your Majesty," she said gently, "you've hardly eaten anything. Don't you like the food?"

"*Like it?*" he roared. "Of course I don't like it. It has been cooked with sugar." He stood up as if to go. "How dare you give a King such food. You have insulted me!"

"Your Majesty, please don't go. Give us one more chance. Try the dishes on this table instead." His daughter beckoned to the table next to his and the king sat down begrudgingly.

He took a mouthful of food from one of the bowls and ate it greedily. Then he smiled. He tried another bowl and then another. The food tasted just right. Why was it, he wondered. He licked his lips thoughtfully and then he knew. *Salt.* The food had been cooked with salt. The King was pleased this time.

Just at that moment, his daughter removed her veil.

"You love salt, don't you?" she said. "You need it every day, much more than you need honey or sugar."

The King stared at his daughter. Who was this girl, he wondered. Then, at last, he realized. She was his own daughter. He could not answer her, for now he knew that her love for him, like salt, was more precious than all the honey and sugar in the world.

"Daughter," said the King, holding out his arms, "forgive me."

The King was ashamed of the way he had treated his daughter. Now he wanted to make up to her for all the wrong he had done. So he gave the young couple his kingdom and they became King and Queen, and they all lived happily together in his palace.